# Thin Ice

by

Chris Powling

Illustrated by Sue Mason

To Ben Kirkwood
A big thank you for helping me with the ending of the story.

**You do not need to read this page – just get on with the book!**

ISBN: 978-1-84299-557-0

Printed in Great Britain by Bell & Bain Ltd

# Contents

# Chapter 1
# The Boss

We had snow on the way.

Lots of snow.

That's what the TV said. That's what the radio said. That's what Mum said as she packed us both off to school.

"Wrap up warm, Pete," she told me, "And you too, Kevin."

SNOW! SNOW! SNOW!

The Boss even talked about it in Assembly. The Boss is the name we give the Head-teacher at our School. His real name is Mr Boston. His hair is so white he looks a bit snowy himself. "Have fun with the snow this week-end," he said. "Throw snow-balls. Make snow-men. Follow snow-tracks. But there's one thing you must never do after a snow-storm ..."

The Boss shut an eye.

He lifted a finger.

He wagged his head from side to side.

He's such a show-off, you see. He loves it when we're all looking at him. He made us wait for about 100 years before he went on. Then, in a voice like thunder, he said *"Stay away from frozen water!"*

"Frozen water, sir?" said one of the new kids.

"Frozen water," said the Boss, grimly.

"Like ice lollies, sir?" the new kid said. "I don't get it. Why must we stay away from ice lollies?"

"Not that kind of frozen water!" the Boss snorted. "I'm talking about lakes and ponds and rivers. I'm talking about the kind of frozen water that can kill you."

He went on and on about it.

About frozen water that cracks under you. About frozen water that's so cold it

stops your heart in mid-beat. "Just think about it," said the Boss. "Under the ice it's like a frozen roof over your head. You're bashing it with your frozen fists. But it's too frozen to shatter from below. So you sink down and down and down and you don't come up again ..."

He let his words hang in the air.

We'd never been so silent in Assembly. If someone had dropped a pin, we would have jumped out of our skins. Even the teachers were gripped. The Boss was enjoying himself.

He shut an eye.

He lifted a finger.

He wagged his head from side to side.

When he spoke next he put on his sternest voice. "How are you feeling now?" he asked.

The Boss was looking at the new kid as he said this. The new kid's eyes were wide with fright. He was really spooked. "Like a big ice-lolly!" he yelped.

# Chapter 2
# What Snow?

OK, I'd better admit it. You'll find out sooner or later, anyway. Remember the new kid who called out in Assembly? The one who was spooked? Well, he's my little brother, Kevin.

And he's a pain. He upsets people, you see. He's such a baby, he just can't help it.

Even the Boss was upset. You could tell that from his face. He stomped out of the hall in a right old temper. The rest of us couldn't stop sniggering. Even the teachers had to hold their hands over their mouths.

Kids were still talking about it at home-time. One would say, "Down and down and down ... and you don't come up again! How are you feeling now?"

Another would yelp, "Like a big ice-lolly!"

Kevin's face went red when he heard this. "I didn't mean to spoil the Boss's Assembly, Pete," he told me.

"Didn't you?" I said.

"No, I didn't. The words just popped out of my mouth."

"The Boss was just showing off," I said.

"So all that stuff he told us wasn't true?"

"Who cares, Kevin?"

"I care," said my little brother. "I care about it a lot. And so will you care if it *snows* ..."

But it didn't snow.

Not when we were walking home. Not when we were eating supper. Not at bath-time. Not even when we were going to bed. The TV, the radio and Mum must have got it all wrong. So much for The Boss and his frozen water.

# Chapter 3
# Oh ... That Snow

Next day I woke up early.

Don't ask me why.

There was no sound in the house. There was no sound from the street, either. Still sleepy, I looked round the room. What had woken me? Maybe it was the white light creeping over my face.

The *white light?*

Now I was in a rush. I jumped out of bed and ran to the big window on the landing. Kevin was there before me. He was tucked up on the window-seat. His nose was pressed against the glass. "Look, Pete!" he said, softly.

WOW!

The park next door had gone as white as the Boss's hair – no, much whiter than that. We were dazzled by it. "Snow-balls, Kevin!" I said. "And snow-men. And don't forget the snow-tracks. We can be the first kids out there!"

"What about Mum and Dad?"

"It's the week-end, OK? They'll stay in bed for hours. By then the snow may have melted."

"Melted?"

"You bet," I said.

And I shut an eye.

I lifted a finger.

I wagged my head from side-to-side.

I was doing my best to copy the Boss. I made Kevin wait for about a 100 years before I spoke again. “How are you feeling now?” I asked him. “Still like a big ice-lolly?”

# Chapter 4
# In the Park

We'd been to the park next door loads of times. But we'd never seen it looking like this. It was like a picture on a Christmas card. No wonder the Boss had told us to have some fun. He was spot-on about that. We chucked snow-balls. We made a snow-man. We even found a snow-track that led deeper into the park. “Are they animal foot-prints, Pete?” Kevin asked.

“Maybe a fox,” I said.

“Or could be some sort of wild-cat. Or a snow-tiger that’s got away from the zoo.”

"A snow-tiger?" I grinned.

I ask you.

Kevin is such a baby.

The foot-prints led us to the top of a hill. Then down the slope on the other side. Soon, we'd got as far as the boating pond. At least, I think it was the boating pond. In the summer it was cool and splashy. It wasn't like that now. For a start, there were no boats. Also, it seemed deeper somehow. It was smoother and harder as well – a bit like our play-ground back at school.

Suddenly, Kevin stood very still. "I know what this is, Pete," he said. "It's frozen water!"

# Chapter 5
# The Pond

It was frozen water all right.

I felt a shiver run down my spine. In summer, the boating pond was magic. You could go for a row if you wanted. You could take out a canoe. You could ride a paddle-boat just like a bike. But in winter the magic stopped. The park keeper packed it all away. The pond was just a pond after that.

*Unless it was solid ice.*

That's how it looked right now. I grabbed Kevin's arm. "What are you goggling at?" I hissed.

"At the dog, Pete."

"What dog?"

"The dog in the middle of the pond."

"Oh ... that dog."

The dog was so small and fluffy I hadn't seen it at first. In fact, I could only just see it now. Was it old or still a puppy? It lay

flat out on the ice at the end of the trail of foot-prints.

Kevin bit his lip. "Is it asleep, Pete?"

"Maybe dead," I said.

"No, it's not dead. It's shivering, can't you see? It must have worn itself out in the snow."

"Maybe it's too afraid to move, Pete."

"Afraid of what?"

I didn't like to tell him. It wasn't a good time to talk about ice that cracks under you. Or water so cold it can stop your heart in mid-beat. OK, so this dog had missed our school Assembly. That didn't mean it was stupid.

My little brother wasn't stupid, either. Words just popped out of his mouth, that's all. "Pete ..." he said, softly.

"Yes, Kevin?"

"You've got to save it, OK?"

*Save it?*

*Me?*

# Chapter 6
# Big Mistake

I looked across the pond. The dog was as still as ever. It had even stopped shivering. Maybe we were too late. But I had to give it a go. If I didn't, I knew who would.

My little brother, Kevin, that's who.

So I broke a stick off a frozen bush nearby ... and I stepped down onto the pond.

OK! OK! OK!

I must have been crazy. The pond wasn't very deep – last summer, in the boat, I kept hitting the bottom with my paddle. Also, the ice under my feet felt as solid as a rock. But I was still doing something stupid. I was in a panic as well.

So I tested the ice with every step.

Tap-tap-tap went my stick on the frozen water. A blind kid could have walked faster, I admit. But at least I got to the dog safe and sound. I bent down to give it a pat.

YAP! YAP! YAP!

It nipped at my fingers. It jumped over my arm. It zipped away like a rocket – all in a nano-second. It shot up the slope on the far side of the pond in a flurry of snow.

That's when I saw the man who'd been calling out for the dog. He saw me at just the same moment. His mouth sagged open in shock. So did mine. I knew who he was at once. It was Mr Boston ... the Boss. His dazzling white hair was hard to miss.

What was the Boss doing in *our* park?

# Chapter 7
# The Boss on Ice

Mr Boston was looking for his little fluffy dog. Or he was till he spotted me.

"Pete?" he snapped.

"Sir?"

“Didn’t you hear what I said in Assembly about frozen water? About the way it can crack under you? About it being so cold it can stop your heart in mid-beat? Were you asleep?”

“No, sir, I heard every word ...”

“So you took no notice?”

“No, sir. It’s just that –”

“Yes?”

I wanted to tell him about the dog. His dog. But I could see it was no good. He had made up his mind what to do. The Boss always knew what to do.

He shut an eye.

He lifted a finger.

He wagged his head from side to side.

When he spoke this time he kept his voice very cool. I think he was afraid I might panic. "Pete," he said. "Don't move. Stay just where you are. That ice may look safe and sound but you mustn't trust it for a moment. I'll come and get you myself."

He was coming to get me *himself?*

It was the last thing I wanted. Another set of feet – Boss-size feet this time – on the frozen pond? That would be the end of both

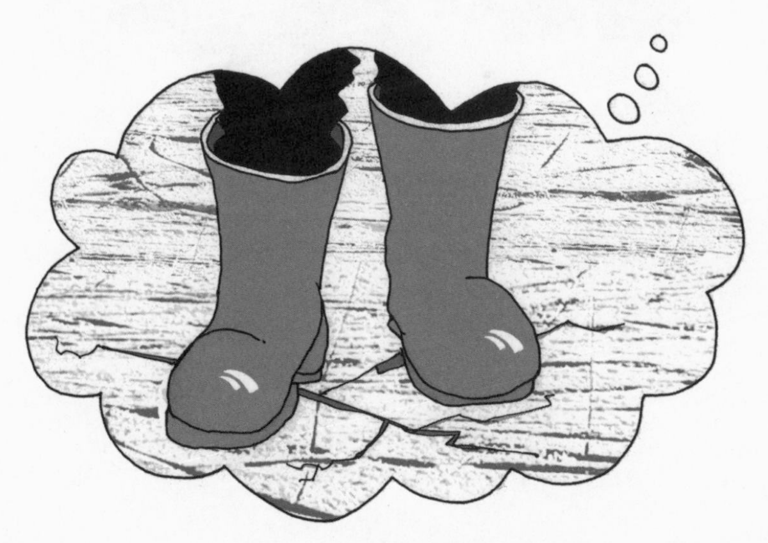

of us. I looked back at Kevin. I could see he was bothered as well.

But what could the two of us do?

The Boss was on his way. He slid quickly down the slope to the edge of the pond. He peered at the ice and nodded. “There’s a trick to this, Pete," he said. "You mustn't stand with all your bulk on one spot. That's what shatters the ice. You've got to spread your body out. Do you understand?"

"I think so, sir."

"Shall I show you?"

"Yes please, sir," I said.

"Like this, OK?"

He got down on his knees. He lowered himself onto the ice in a sort of star-shape. Then, using his fingers and toes to get a grip, he started to shuffle my way on his tummy. I have to tell you it looked a bit weird. He'd never done this in Assembly. I could hear Kevin snuffling a bit. I think he was trying not to giggle.

So was I.

It's hard *not* to giggle when your Head-teacher is creeping your way on his tummy.

He was worn out by the time he got to me. "That's how you do it, Pete," he puffed.

"Is it, sir?"

"You'll find it in all the books."

He rolled onto his back, still panting. The ice and snow from the pond was stuck to the front of his coat. It was as if some of his hair had fallen out from shock. "Shall we go back, then?" he asked.

"The way you did, sir?"

"How else?" said the Boss. "You can't be too careful when it comes to ice."

“What about them, sir?” Kevin called from the side of the pond.

“Them?”

“Those big kids at the top of the hill ... they don’t look very careful to me.”

Kevin pointed.

There were three big kids up there. They were sitting on a huge sled. It was already on the move. On the move? *It was pelting down the slope at top speed.* They were coming right at us. Any second now the sled would smash onto the ice like a bomb-shell ... with all its bulk on one spot.

# Chapter 8
# Down and Down and Down

The Boss didn't make a sound.

Nor did I.

How can you speak when you're stiff with terror? We simply goggled at the looming sled. The closer it came, the bigger it looked. So did the three kids riding it. They

seemed to hover over the pond for about 100 years.

Then the sled crashed on the ice in front of us.

KA-BOOM!

The three big kids got off at once. Close-up, they were bigger than ever – at least Year 9. They gave the Boss a puzzled look.

"Hello, sir," one of them said. "Long time no see. What are you doing here? Is it one of your drama projects?"

"Something like that," the Boss choked.

"Don't catch cold, sir!"

"I won't."

They stomped back up the slope with the sled. At the top, they swung round. Then they lined up for another go. I gazed down at the ice. How come it was so solid? The sled had landed like a ton of bricks. But it hadn't even left a dent.

Was this some kind of super-ice?

No, it wasn't.

Suddenly, I worked it out. It wasn't ice at all. *It was only a coating of snow on the bottom of the empty pond.*

In Winter, the park keeper doesn't just pack up the boats and stuff. He drains the water away as well.

I heard the Boss give a dry chuckle. "Fooled the two of you there, didn't I?" he said.

"Yes, sir," I said.

"Have you both learned a lesson today?"

"You bet, sir," said Kevin.

And so we had. But had he?

*We'd* learned about the dangers of frozen water. Had the *Boss* also learned about the dangers of showing off?

Barrington Stoke would like to thank all its readers for commenting on the manuscript before publication and in particular:

Tim Andrews
Scott Evison
Bronte Harris
Peter King
Ben Kirkwood
Frederick Lange
Alex Langton
Rachel Langton
Pieter Lap
Tommy Lee
Paul Maddon
Rebecca Metton
Dhena Patel
Harry Penrice
Kieron Skelton
Lea Smith
Naomi Shepherd
Freddie Stebbings
Giacomo Sumner
Laura Waugh

**Become a Consultant!**

Would you like to give us feedback on our titles before they are published? Contact us at the email address below – we'd love to hear from you!

info@barringtonstoke.co.uk
www.barringtonstoke.co.uk

Ready for more? Try ...

# *Snow Dogs*

**by**

**Jane A. C. West**

Zeb wants to win the dog sled race.
But will he die before he gets
to the end?

Ready for more? Try ...

# *United, Here I Come!*

**by**

**Alan Combes**

Joey and Jimmy are very bad at football. But Jimmy is sure he will play for United one day. Is Jimmy crazy – or will he get there?